# Curious George
## Apple Harvest

**Adaptation by Lynne Polvino**
**Based on the TV series teleplay written by Chuck Tately**

Houghton Mifflin Harcourt Publishing Company
Boston    New York

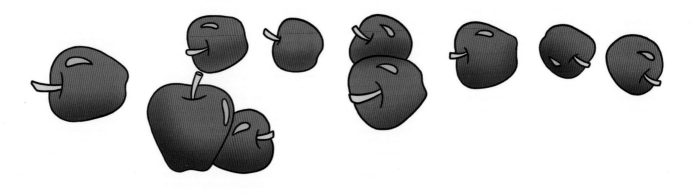

For information about permission to reproduce selections from this book, write to Permissions, Houghton Mifflin Harcourt Publishing Company, 215 Park Avenue South, New York, New York 10003.

Library of Congress Cataloging-in-Publication Data is on file.

ISBN: 978-0-547-51705-6
Design by Afsoon Razavi
www.hmhbooks.com
Printed in China
LEO 10 9 8 7 6 5 4 3 2
4500400685

It was harvest time, and Mr. Renkins needed help picking his apples. George and his friend the man with the yellow hat were happy to lend a hand . . .

or foot! Mr. Renkins explained that they needed to collect every apple.

"I'm going to join the missus 'round back," he said. "Once you fill that cart, you can unload it into the washing trough."

Mr. Renkins took his cart full of apples to the barn and dumped them into the water. It must be their bath time, George thought.

George climbed up the branches, collected the shiny red apples in his friend's hat, and put them into the cart. What fun! High up in the tree, he saw Jumpy Squirrel picking apples, too.

George decided to help. He took Jumpy's apple and tossed it into the cart with the rest of Mr. Renkins's apples. But Jumpy wanted that apple for himself! He leaped in to take it back, and George tried to stop him.

"Easy now, George. That lever releases all of the apples," said his friend. George looked at the lever.

He thought it was an excellent way to get Jumpy out of the cart.

"George! No!"

George pulled the lever and Jumpy tumbled out—along with all of the apples!

"That's okay," said his friend with a sigh. "We can gather them up again." But Jumpy had found his apple, and he ran to hide it in the barn. George decided to follow.

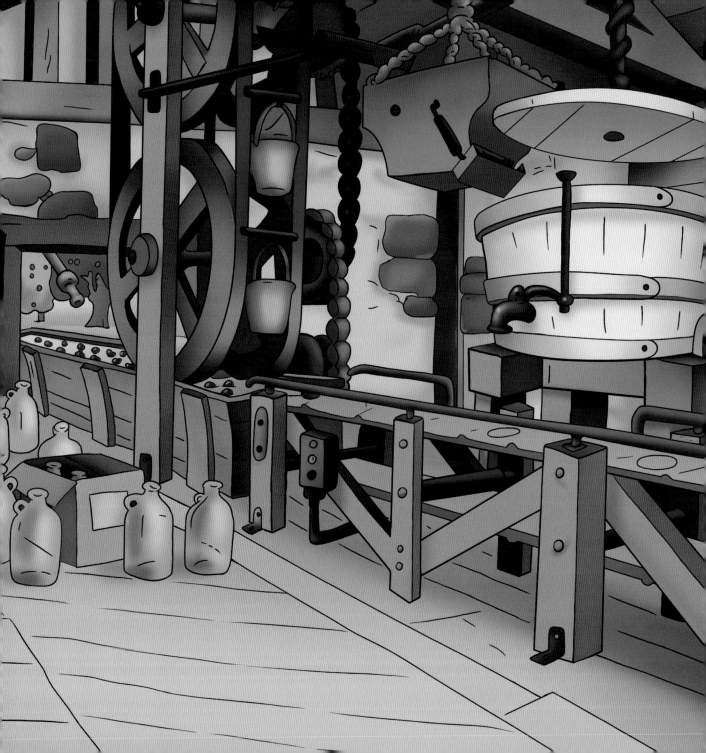

George looked around the
inside of the barn in wonder.
There were all sorts of things to
climb on and swing from. It must
be some kind of monkey playground!

But George was not here to play. He had
to get that apple from Jumpy. If only it
weren't so dark in the barn. He found the light switch and flipped it.

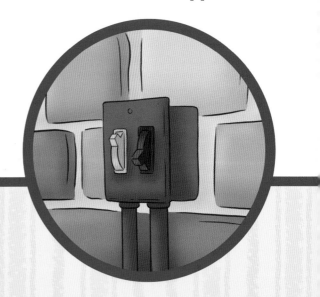

Everything moved! It was a machine, not a playground. George wondered how it worked. He watched the buckets scoop up the apples. He decided they must carry the apples high away from squirrels. But, wait—where was Jumpy?

There he was! Jumpy still had the apple he took from the cart. George chased Jumpy, grabbed the apple, and threw it into a bin high out of reach. Suddenly the machine stopped.

George found a button and pushed. The machine started again! This time all of the parts started working, including the moving belt. But when he looked up, he saw all of the Renkinses' beautiful apples being chopped to bits! The chopped-up apples dropped into a giant barrel, and a lid was lowered tightly on top of them.

Too tightly! Liquid began to pour out of the barrel. What a mess! George had an idea. He ran up and put his mouth under the liquid. It tasted good—a lot like apples. But there was too much of it. Luckily, he saw some empty containers.

George scrambled to put the containers on the moving belt fast enough to catch the liquid.

Then he looked down at the end of the belt and saw the containers falling onto the floor. Uh-oh. George ran to catch them. Then he needed to stop the machine!

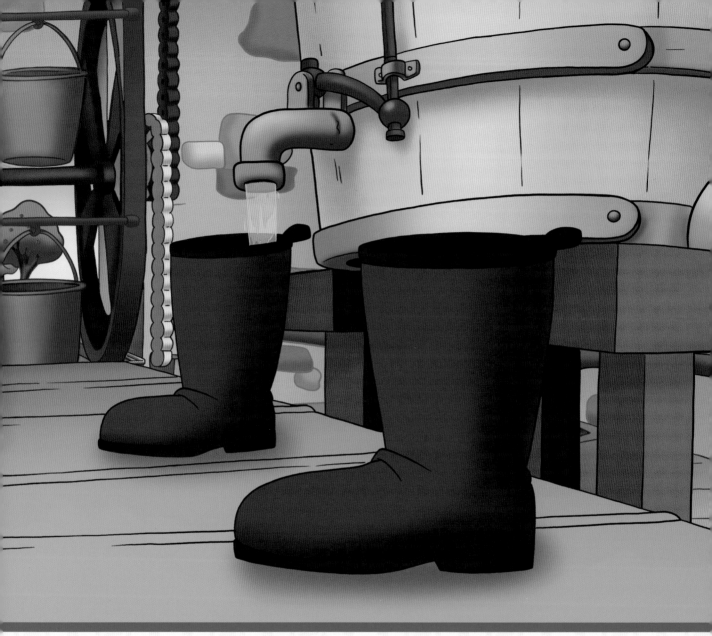

Soon he had filled all of the containers, but the golden liquid continued to pour ou
He looked around for another container and saw a big pair of rubber boots.

As the last boot was filled, the liquid stopped pouring out and the machine stopped. Whew! The farmers and George's friend appeared in the doorway.

"Well, I'll be!" Mr. Renkins exclaimed.

George froze. The Renkinses would surely be upset that he ruined all of their apples.

"George!" Mrs. Renkins rushed up to him. "You've done a fantastic job. All that cider already pressed and bottled? Thank you!"

"This is some machine," said the man with the yellow hat.
"See, the apples are washed here," Mrs. Renkins explained.

"Then they are lifted up to the chopper, because chopped apples give more juice. The juice is pressed out of the apples, and then bottled."

George had not ruined the apples after all! He'd turned them into cider!

Mr. Renkins handed an apple to George. "Here, you've earned it," he said. George knew someone who wanted the apple more than he did. He'd had enough apples for one day!

# Assembly Line

**When George accidentally turned on the cider press, he learned how cider is made. In each step, a different part of the machine performs a specific task, and when all of the steps are put together, the end result is bottled cider. This process is called an assembly line. Assembly lines allow companies to make their products faster, cheaper, and more evenly. If George had tried to do each step of the cider-making assembly line by himself, it would have taken a lot longer to fill all of those bottles of cider!**

**Below are the tasks each part of the cider press machine performed to make cider. Can you number them in the correct order?**

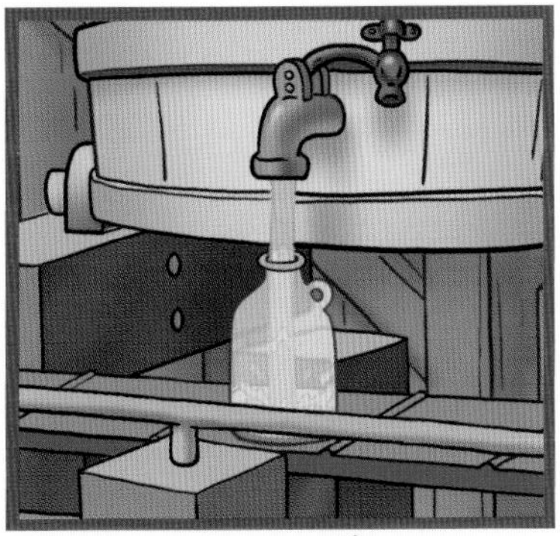

**Step** 6

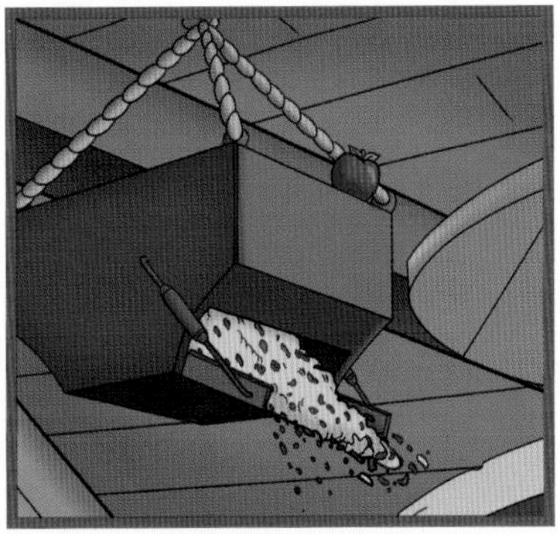

**Step** 5

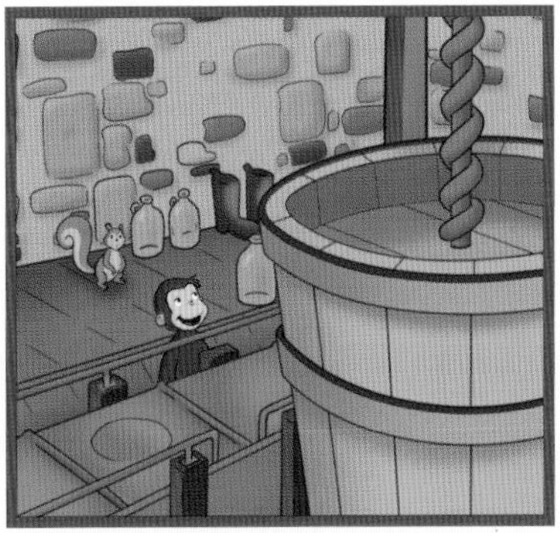

**Step** 4

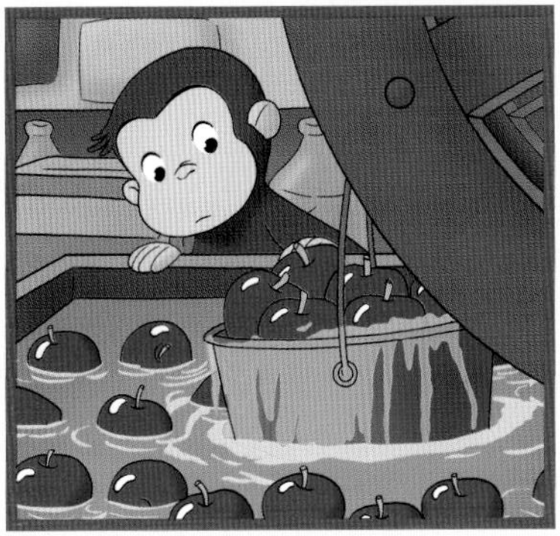

**Step** 3

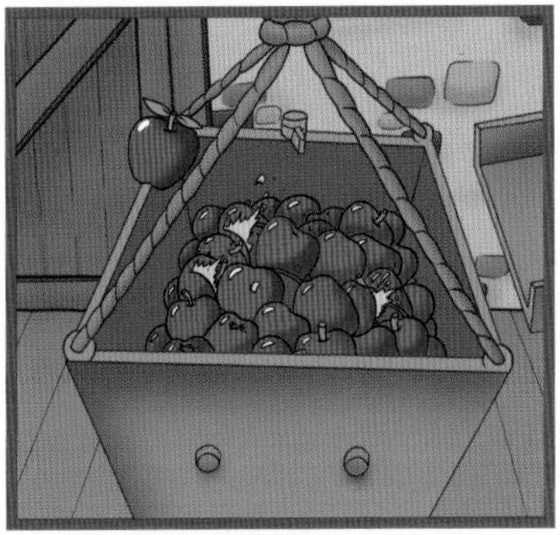

**Step** 2

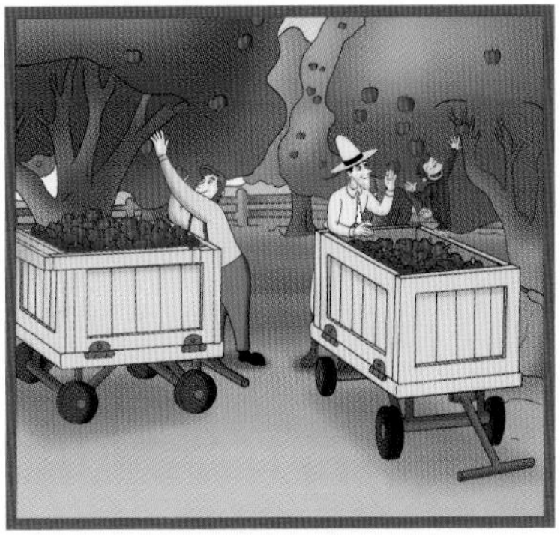

**Step** 1

**ANSWERS: Top (left to right): 6, 4, 5; bottom (left to right) 2, 3, 1**

## Apple Stars

Did you know that a star is hidden inside each and every apple? Next time you're having apple slices for a snack, ask an adult to cut the apple horizontally across the middle instead of vertically from the stem to the base. Inside each apple half you will find a star!

## Apple Smiles

Cider isn't the only thing you can make out of apples! Apple pies, apple sauce, apple butter, and candied apples are just a few of the many treats that can be made with this delicious fruit. With the help of an adult, you can even make apple smiles. Here's how:

### Ingredients:
2 sliced red apples
peanut butter or cream cheese
mini marshmallows

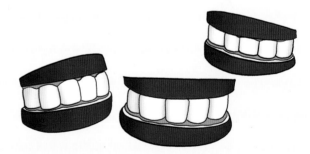

### Directions:

1. Ask an adult to cut the red apples into slices (these are the lips).

2. Spread peanut butter or cream cheese on top of two apple slices.

3. Place mini marshmallows (these are the teeth) on top of peanut butter or cream cheese, and top with another apple slice.